A GOTHIC SHORT STORY COLLECTION

I0456883

The MACABRE LIFE of LIA GRIMSLI

Daphne Paige

To all the Scorpios born with a need for something

spooky

&

To Papa, who shares my love of the macabre

A GOTHIC SHORT STORY COLLECTION

The MACABRE LIFE of LIA GRIMSLI

Warning: This book contains acts of violence, reanimation of the dead, and other macabre behavior

Contents

Welcome Athelia Grimsli

A woman is lying in a hospital bed. The white sheets are plastered to her skin with sweat, and her blonde hair is stuck to the back of her neck and matted around her head. The soft beeping of the machine beside her parallels with the soft whine of the newborn in the father's hands.

Robert Grimsli looks from the small face of the baby he's holding with nearly black eyes and straight black hair, to his wife, whose hair is the color of sunshine. His little girl, Athelia, must take after him.

Robert sits down in the chair at his wife's side, cradling his baby girl in his arms. He's always wanted a child who could follow in his footsteps, but he always pictured having a little boy. *A girl?* He hopes she takes after him in more ways than just her appearance. He'll need someone to pass his legacy to when his time comes. Someone to continue his work long after he's buried in the ground.

He tilts his head, ignoring whatever mumbo-jumbo his wife is saying, to study his daughter's eyes. He can always tell if they have *it* by looking into their eyes. Athelia tilts her head too, copying her father's movements. Her coal-black eyes stare back at him with an intensity that makes his skin prickle. *That's it. She has it.*

His thin lips twist into an unsettling smile. This little girl may be his greatest creation yet—which is saying something, considering the numerous awards hanging on his office wall.

Robert Grimsli is a scientist; a *world-renowned* scientist, as he likes to clarify. And ever since his career began, he's wanted to accomplish one specific thing: he wants to defy death. To reanimate the dead. To create an elixir of immortality.

So far, he hasn't succeeded. Though he has picked up quite a following of similarly minded, *lesser* scientists and *fiction geeks*. Every time he sees one of those…people…with a shirt spouting some fictitious garbage and a bent-up novel clutched in their greasy hand, he wants to roll his eyes to the ceiling. They always seem to infiltrate his conferences, no matter how many times he tells the ticket-keepers to deny access to anyone who looks mentally unstable. They come up to him, saying something nonsensical about Dracula or Frankenstein. What he's doing isn't a fantasy. It's science. Pure, bold, emblazoned science. And one day, with the help of his brilliant Athelia, everyone will realize that.

He smooths her pitch-black hair, bringing

3

her forehead up to his puckered lips. *His* Athelia. His brilliant little scientist.

"Darling?" his wife asks, for probably the hundredth time. Her face is etched with concern. "Can I hold her?" She holds her hands out for the baby, eyebrows drawn over her eyes and lips slightly pouty. Robert frowns but reluctantly hands her Athelia.

"She's going to be just like me," he declares, focusing on Athelia's face. Her tiny eyes squint over at him as if she understands what he's saying.

His wife doesn't respond at first, so he snaps his head up to look at her, searching for confirmation. He scowls when he notices the knot of dread that has slipped across her brow.

His wife cradles Athelia to her chest, studying the baby girl's dark eyes. Robert watches a bead of sweat slip down her temple. She must see *it* too. The desire for power already embedded in their beautiful little girl. Just like him.

A smile curls his lips as he watches his baby

girl, realizing that it's up to him to form her future. To turn her into his little scientist. His beautiful, talented, wicked little girl.

Athelia Rose Grimsli.

Lia Grimsli and the Unsuspecting Worm

Lia squints down at the worm wiggling in the dirt, her nose scrunched in concentration. The worm is nearly the same terracotta color as the dry dirt around it.

"What do you think it's searching for?" Henry asks, squatting in front of Lia. His worn leather shoes tamp down the brittle grass.

Lia grabs a small twig in the grass and

slides it under the worm, lifting it out of the dirt. It writhes on the end of the stick, and Lia's cracked lips twist into a smile. "Food probably. Or maybe it's looking for its family. I saw a few worms squished on the sidewalk over there."

"Oh…" Henry pouts. "Poor thing."

"Should we go show it?" Lia suggests, her smile turning malicious.

Henry shrinks away from his older sister. Kneeling on dirt and tiny rocks leaves little indents on his knees and his skin red. His sandy-brown eyebrows lower over his eyes, and his pout intensifies. "Athelia…"

Lia glares at him. "Lia. You know better than to call me that." She spits the last word with venom.

Henry cowers. "Lia, sorry." He shakes his head, his dull eyes losing any trace of rebellion.

"I think it wants to go see its family," Lia sing-songs, each word dripping with malice. Her dark eyes shine with the thought of upsetting her brother; sure, she loves him, but seeing him squirm brings her so much joy—love in comparison is nothing.

"Please, Lia," Henry whines, watching as his sister stands up from the grass. Her faded gray dress falls just above her ankles, now covered in grass stains. Her black high-tops are laced tightly, and her black hair falls loosely down her back.

"Don't do it, Lia," Henry insists, following her as she heads out of their yard and toward the sidewalk that borders the left side of their suburban home. There's a window in the middle of the side of the house that's framed with buttery yellow curtains. Lia can just make out the neatly brushed blonde hair of her mother. She must be making lunch.

Lia stops beneath the window; she's about two feet too short to see inside from this close, but an idea is blossoming in her mind. She glances down at the squished worms patterning the sidewalk at her feet, little pink and brown bits smeared on the gray ground. The worm is still dangling from the end of her stick, draped over it like a horseshoe. She wonders if it recognizes the distant, misshapen bodies of its family, or if it's just a brainless worm incapable of memory or emotion.

"Hold this," Lia orders, thrusting the stick toward Henry, whose eyes are rimmed with red and watery, as if he's forcing back tears. The boy should really grow a backbone, let alone a sense of humor.

"Why? What are you going to do?" he begs, taking hold of the end of the stick and watching the poor worm wiggle. His lips turn down, and his long black eyelashes paint matching shadows across his pale cheeks.

Lia glares at him. Why must he be so annoying? Daddy teaches them never to ask questions when he's doing his scientific experiments downstairs in the basement. She needs to teach Henry to abide by the same rules when it comes to her own experiments.

"Just wait here. I'll be back."

She leaves Henry pouting to himself at the edge of the side yard. She finds the back door to their bland, tan house. Being weary of her mother's precious vegetable garden on either side of the door, she creaks it open and steps inside. The smell of roasted asparagus and baked cheesy potatoes hits her instantly, making her mouth water. She shakes her head, reminding herself that scientists don't get distracted by silly things such as food. They eat once they're done with their experiments.

The small, faux-crystal chandelier dangling from the ceiling cloaks the room in warm, welcoming light. She scowls. She prefers the harsh fluorescence in the basement, but her mother has always been over the top. Daddy let her furnish the house on the condition that the basement is his alone.

Mom turns around from the sink, where she was chopping off the ends of carrots. Her cheery smile instantly repulses Lia.

"Athelia, baby. What are you and Henry up to?" she asks, wrapping an arm around Lia's shoulders and tugging her into a one-sided hug. "Lunch is going to be ready in about half an hour. Think you both can be inside by then?"

Lia pulls away from her mother's embrace, her skin pricking with the touch of someone who's so...*sweet*. So sweet it's sickening. Where's Daddy and his cold, impersonal demeanor?

Lia ignores her mother's questions, instead searching for the very item she came inside to find. Her eyes brighten when they land on the little wooden block on the far counter, black handles poking out, just waiting for her to reach out and claim one. She skirts around her mother, knowing that if she caught on to what Lia has planned, she'd put an immediate stop to it. She just doesn't understand science.

Lia grabs the handle of a small knife. She doesn't know exactly what type it is, but all she needs to know is that it's sharp and it'll do the job.

Her mother starts to hum, completely unaware of Lia's diabolical plan. Diabolical and brilliant, if she says so herself.

She walks back outside, a smirk twisting up her lips. Before she even turns the corner, she's explaining her plan to her brother, assuming he can hear. "Henry…this is most exciting! Have you heard that worms that get split in two actually survive? And can regrow? We're about to find out!" She turns the corner, and her smirk instantly drops. "Henry…" She glowers.

Her brother is standing in the middle of the sidewalk, his arms crossed, and a defiant expression on his face that slowly starts to fade. He uncrosses his arms and seems to shrink in on himself.

But Lia doesn't care about her brother's obvious lack of confidence. The only thing she cares about is…

"Where did you put the worm, Henry?" She arcs an eyebrow.

Drop of Nightshade

Lia Grimsli has never gotten along with her mother. Mother's too happy, cheerful, and smiley... All the time. It grates under Lia's skin like an incurable infection. Lia can tell that it does the same to Daddy—either that or the contortion of his face when he lays his eyes on Mother is that of love. Lia supposes she wouldn't know either way.

There's a garden far beyond her family's

home, past the reach of the forked branches bordering the tree line, and just behind the Gate of Shadows—the name for the ominous collection of darkness in the thick of the forest, given by scaredy-cat Henry, of course. And in this hidden garden is an unruly, blooming conglomeration of nightshade. Purple petals reach toward the treetops, and black berries dangle, ready to be plucked by Lia's determined little hands.

Lia loves this garden more than almost anything. Here, she can be alone. Surrounded by the life of plants that can't cower in fear or call her harsh words or smile all brightly. They can poison and heal and consume, but they cannot talk to her, which is what she usually comes here to seek. But today, she stops in the middle of the thicket and examines the bushes of nightshade that blossom in the heat of summer.

She can get rid of her mother and finally cure that infection under her skin. But she cannot regret it. If she regretted it, then she

16

couldn't live her life to the fullest. Always held back by a decision of her childhood. She's only eight, and even though the decision should be hard, she barely gives it more than a minute of contemplation.

With her grubby little hand, she reaches up and plucks a handful of nightshade, sealing her mother's fate and forging the path to her future.

The Early Intrigue of Lia Grimsli

Lia Grimsli hurries behind her father; a tall, lean man with thinning white hair. His footsteps are loud on the marble flooring. The fluorescent lights dangling from the ceiling above them cast the entirety of the hallway in an obnoxiously bright light.

Lia knows better than to ask her father where he's going. But by the dark leather notebook held tight against his side, she knows it's for one of his *experiments*. Experiments she's dreamed of witnessing, of taking part in. Her mother banned her from even speaking to Father about his work, calling it acts of the Devil, *witchcraft*. Though Lia has always known that science is called by cruel, inaccurate terms. Science is what her father lives for. What he's renowned for.

Lia's lips contort into a rather maniacal smile, especially for an eight-year-old girl, knowing that her mother can't prevent her from following in her father's footsteps any longer. Mother has gone *away*. One drop of nightshade and Lia secured her place beside the fabled Doctor Grimsli.

Her father stops abruptly in front of a stark white door at the end of the hallway. He clears his throat, raises his hand to knock, and scowls as the door flies open before his knuckles even make contact. "Perkins." His tone is one of dismay. "I was told you wouldn't be assisting today."

Lia peeks around her father at the woman

who's taller than most, with hair as bright as blood, and skin as pale as the walls around them. A pair of thick, red glasses sits perched on her angular nose, and her face twists with a matching scowl. "And I was told a different scientist was coming to take a look." Her brown eyes flit down and snag on Lia, one eyebrow raising of its own accord. "A child? You brought a *child* into a morgue?"

Father clears his throat again. "Lia wanted to see. Is that a problem, Perkins?" His voice begs her to challenge him, flaunting his superiority, and his title of *Ground-Breaking Scientist of the Year*. A title rightfully given. Lia may not know what her father does, but she knows how genius he is.

Perkins swallows, casts a doubtful glance at the small girl half-hidden behind her father's legs, then steps aside. "Jane Doe is waiting on table three."

Father leads Lia into the room, stride as precise and confident as a practiced hand with a scalpel. He stops at the head of a metal table,

21

and the room smells distinctly clean, *too* clean, though there's an underlay of musk. Riper the closer Lia stands to the table. A table as tall as her, preventing her from seeing what has caught her father's attention.

"Bring her a chair," Father demands, not bothering to look up from the table. He brings the notebook up to his face, skimming through a few pages before producing a fountain pen from his jacket pocket.

"Are you sure?" Perkins hesitantly asks. With a stern glare from Father, she hurries to fetch a chair from behind the desk at the far end of the smelly room. She brings it back to Lia, face ghostly white as the little girl climbs onto it, finally getting a look at what has caught her father's intrigue.

Father passes the fountain pen and the notebook to Lia, whose eyes bore down on the lifeless body of a so-called Jane Doe. A white sheet covers her from her collarbone down. "Write down what I say. Understand, Lia?" Father asks, calculating gaze now set on his daughter's soft features.

Lia pries her eyes away from the body and focuses on the notebook. Inked depictions of cuts and human organs, of the skeletal and muscular system, sprawl across the pressed cream pages. Notes are written in her father's hasty handwriting. She lifts the pen with a steady hand, flips through the pages until she finds a blank one, and waits eagerly for her father to begin.

He leans over the Jane Doe, tracing the faint cuts and scars on her face with his nearly black eyes. "Jane Doe. Caucasian. Five foot three. Brown hair." He forces open her eyes. "Blue eyes." With a sniff, he determines, "Twenty-four hours old." He takes a step back and tilts his head to the side. Lia can practically see the gears in his head turning, steam billowing from his ears. "Sheep will do. Living."

Lia, with eyebrows drawn and mouth curved downward, scrawls in looping letters everything her father has said. Though she doesn't understand much, she can feel the absolute brilliance weighted in her father's statements.

"Sheep? You tried pig last time. That didn't work. What makes you think a sheep will?" Perkins asks. Lia understands now why her father doesn't like this woman. She asks too many questions and judges every decision he makes. *She* doesn't understand science. Not truly.

"If something doesn't work, Perkins," Father chides, "you try something else. One sheep. Young. The heartbeat has to be fast. I want it by morning. The cadaver can't wait much longer or it'll be far past its prime."

Perkins sighs and nods. "I'll alert you when the delivery arrives."

Lia and her father leave the stale scent of the morgue behind, footsteps paired on the floor and shadows drawn out in front of them as they reach the section where the fluorescent lights are behind them.

Finally, Father breaks the stretching silence. "Lia, do you know what my goal is?"

The little girl tilts her head up at her father. "Your goal?" she asks, voice squeaky with youth.

"Yes," he sighs, drawing in a sharp breath. "The one goal that all my research is driving me toward."

"What is it, Daddy?" Lia tries to quell her hunger for what he has to say. What does father get up to late at night, hunched over the bodies of dead women and requesting the delivery of live animals?

"To create an elixir for immortality," he says. Lia can hear the grin in his voice, the *pride* ending every syllable. "But first, we need to bring the dead back to life. Now don't we?" He winks down at his daughter. "I've tried every common animal with a big enough brain and heart to animate a human. None of them were a success. But I have a feeling about this one." He opens the metal doors leading to a dimly lit back-alley. Lia knows that if she follows the alley toward the main road, crosses the street and walks for two blocks, she'll arrive home—

where her brother, Henry, is waiting.

"Let's just keep this between you and me," Father insists, taking the notebook from Lia's hands. "One day, my darling, this will be yours." He taps his index finger on the leather cover.

"Why won't it be Henry's too?"

Father shakes his head wearily. "Henry isn't like you and me. He takes after your mother more. He won't like what science requires."

"What does science require?" Lia asks.

Father stops in the eerie light of a lamppost and smiles. "Resilience, my darling."

"And do I have resilience, Daddy?" Lia asks, eyes as wide as dinner plates.

Father stoops down, cups her chin, his black eyes meeting her own. "You're me. Small, female, youthful. But still me."

Lia beams at her father's appraisal. She wants to be like him more than *anything*. "Am I joining you tomorrow morning? I want to see if it works."

Father straightens back up. The lamplight

casts a long shadow across his face. "Not this time. I have no doubt how ready you are for this, but I can't afford to have a distraction. Science is too precise." He catches her wilting expression and sighs. "When I get home, you'll know if it worked just by looking at me."

The next day, her father's face is creased with a frown, disappointment written in the steep curve of his hunched form. He doesn't say much as he passes Lia, who is standing in the doorway to the dining room, eager for some explanation of what went wrong. What he does say, however, is: "We'll try again, my darling. Until it works."

Doctor Grimsli

Lia Grimsli looks down at the glass bottle in her hand, a smile slowly forming on her lips. Her brother, Henry, sits on a creaky stool at the messy black table across from her. His fingers curl under the stool's edge, and his usually disheveled hair is highlighted by the golden glow coming from the lantern beside him. The only window in the room looks out on a forest of green treetops and dark sky, the

29

moon offering an unearthly glow to the tools spread across the table. A chilly breeze drifts into the room, raising the hairs on Lia's arms. She swirls the bottle, watching the inky liquid stain the glass with every movement.

"Do you think this is it?" Henry asks, an excited edge creeping into his voice. His light brown eyes glint with mischief.

Lia smirks, holding the bottle up to the lantern. She inspects the shifting colors of the liquid and the little specks that glitter like stars. "Hopefully. I've done everything by the book."

"But even Father couldn't get it," Henry adds, giving her a doubtful look.

Lia sets the bottle down, then scrunches her nose at her brother. She pivots away from the table, crossing the room to a brighter section, illuminated by the blinding fluorescent light.

A steel table sits directly under the long rectangular light, and on it, covered by a white sheet, is a man whose name she doesn't know. Nor does she care to find out what it is. His name is trivial, just like his existence up until this moment. Today, however, he's going to go down in history alongside the brilliant Grimsli family.

"Hello," Lia purrs, tearing the sheet away from the man's face. His groggy brown eyes open, and fear instantly overtakes him. He tries to squirm away from her, but the leather straps pinning him to the operation table are too strong.

"Who are you?" he asks, shaking his head. An attempt, most likely, to deny that this is really happening. That he's trapped under the inspection of a strange teenage girl.

"My name is Lia Grimsli," Lia answers, grinning at the man. Her name—unlike his—is *very* important. It always has been; her father made it so.

"Grimsli? As in—"

"Yes. As in him. Doctor Robert Grimsli." Lia clicks her tongue, tapping the tips of her finely sharpened nails on the steel table.

The wheels of the shorter steel table beside her creak as Henry begins to arrange the necessary tools.

The siblings share a look. Henry nods. "What's your name—" he begins, turning to the man.

Lia glares at her brother. "His name is not important."

"But it will be, sister," Henry says, feigning a rather docile expression.

Lia considers his words. With a blunt nod, she allows him to continue.

The man grits his teeth, straining to free himself of his leather confines.

Henry presses down on the man's chest, and he stills. With an eerily calm voice, Henry says, "That won't work. I'd rather you stop trying."

"And I'd rather you let me go!" the man shouts, throwing his head back against the table. The sound of his skull hitting the steel sends shivers down Lia's spine. Her fingers twitch for the comfort of her operating tools: a scalpel, a needle, perhaps even a bone saw.

"We should begin." Lia gestures to the full moon high in the night sky. Father always said the best experiments are done under the light of a full moon. It's a tradition of sorts, as odd as it may be.

"You're right," Henry agrees, stepping away from the operating table with his hands interlaced behind his back.

"What is she going to do?" the man asks desperately, eyeing Lia as she approaches. Her coal-black hair swishes against the leather apron she dons.

"You know of our father's experiments, don't you?" Lia asks, tilting her head. The man's pale face is sticky with sweat.

He gulps. "Everyone knows of Crazy Doctor Grimsli."

Lia narrows her eyes, tired of hearing her father's brilliance insulted. "He's not crazy."

"Eternal life? It goes against our creator."

Lia removes a pair of matching surgical gloves from the tool table, snapping them onto her hands. "The bottle, Henry."

Henry's footsteps drift toward the black table, then return, the only sound besides the man's panicked breathing.

She takes the bottle from her brother's outstretched hand. The sleek glass bottle containing her father's greatest experiment brings her comfort just by sight alone.

"That can't be—"

"It is."

The man moves his head toward the farther side of the table. "You can't make me drink that! Have you seen what's happened to everyone who has?"

Lia grimaces. "Of course I have."

"Don't make me drink that. Please. You can't," he begs, tears now cascading down his cheeks.

Lia sighs. "That's not a choice right now."

"Why?"

"Because our father's name has to be cleared," Lia responds, taking a step closer to the table. She leans over the stranger, hovering the bottle of swirling midnight above his face. "I will not let him go down in history as crazy."

The man scoffs. "You'll go down with him.

The both of you." He juts his chin toward Henry, who is lurking just within reach of the shadows.

"Hold him," Lia demands. Henry steps into the light, pinching open the man's mouth and wrapping his arm around his head to still him.

"Wait! Wait!" the stranger shouts, attempting again to wriggle free. Henry tightens his arm around his throat, cutting off his air supply. "Dan Wordsworth."

"What?" Henry asks, letting him breathe again.

"That's my name. Just, please, don't let me die nameless."

Henry frowns, and Lia catches a glimpse of weakness in his light brown eyes. Lia tilts her chin up. "Henry?"

He looks away. From his side profile, Lia can see his Adam's apple bob. "Do it."

"I will." She tilts the contents of the bottle into Dan's mouth, staining his tongue black. His wriggling suddenly stops, and his eyes still on the light dangling above them.

Hope flares in Lia's chest. Maybe this time they've actually done it... Maybe, after years of trial and error, her father's name will finally be cleared. Everyone will know how genius he actually was.

The white sheets covering the lower half of Dan suddenly begin to heat up, bursting into flames around the edges, furling inward as they turn to ash, exposing the body beneath.

Dan's skin begins to turn red, vessels of blood bursting throughout the entirety of his body. Then, his flesh begins to melt, sliding off the bone, now bleached white by the contents of the bottle. The slippery masses of crimson land on the table, sizzling like water dropped in hot oil. The stench is the most horrific part. You'd assume it would be the sight of a man melting before you, disintegrating until he no longer resembles even a human—but Lia and Henry have seen it several times before. Volunteer—in the loosest term possible—number six, apparently, is not going down in history.

Dan Wordsworth is still a name without

significance.

Henry tears his eyes away from the sight, trying to hide the tears threatening to drip down his face. He's always been weak, not having the stomach to perform such experiments. That's why their father's notebook was left to Lia, in hopes that she would finish what he started.

Lia pulls a bin out from underneath the operating table. And with her gloved hand, she slides the remnants of the stranger into the bin. She rests her palms on the table and smiles at her brother, smothering her anger for another experiment gone wrong.

"Henry," she calls. Her brother hesitantly looks over at her. "Bring me number seven."

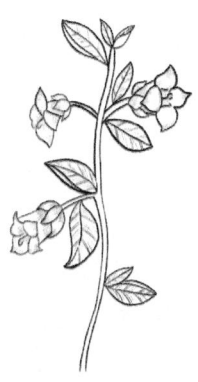

Lia Grimsli and the Wonder of Manipulation

Lia stares across the field at her brother, Henry, and a petite, blonde cheerleader: *Amalie*. She crosses her arms and leans against the edge of the metal bleacher behind her, ignoring the squeak of surprise from the row she's now invading. She squints, her mind scanning over all the possibilities of why Amalie seems so infatuated with Henry. She knows it can't be out of romance. From what she's heard in the women's locker room during physical education, Amalie is a snake of a girl. Which means she's using Henry somehow. Lia is determined to get to the bottom of it.

"Popcorn for five dollars?" a chipper teen with a red and yellow striped apron calls, stopping at the end of Lia's row. He lifts his metal tray toward her, showing her the paper bags of greasy popcorn spilling onto the tray. No one would make the mistake of referring to Lia as a *polite, civilized* girl. Her lip curls in disgust, and she throws the teenage boy a demeaning glare. His lips thin into a grimace, and he hurries to the next row, graciously accepting an outstretched five-dollar bill from a waving hand.

When a round of giggles parts the air and draws Lia's attention to the opposite end of the bleachers, her lips twist into a smirk. With languid limbs, she slips unsuspectingly over to the group of girls, planting a conspiratorial smile on her face. When she sits down on the outskirts of their group, they cast curious glances over at her, wondering what the strange, gothic girl is doing so close to them.

Lia crosses one leg over the other and leans toward them, tilting her head to let her long, black hair fall over her shoulder. "Are you guys friends with Amalie?"

The brunette girl, who seems to be the center of this group, lifts her chin. "Of course we are! Why do *you* want to know?" She raises an eyebrow.

Lia clicks her tongue, sliding her eyes over to her brother and Amalie on the other side of the field. He's leaning over the railing, playing with one of Amalie's blonde braids. From here, Lia can see his heart eyes—which makes her stomach revolt. Her brother is so gullible. Amalie isn't following him around and tagging along to all the events he goes to because she *likes* him. There *has* to be another reason. The Grimslis have *never* been known as likable people. So, *what does she want?*

Lia purposefully leaves them wondering for

longer than necessary. "Is she dating that boy?" She nods toward the two of them at the fence. She doubts they know *'that boy'* is her brother. No one cares about Lia or Henry enough to make that connection. Besides, it's harder to draw a connection between her and Henry since they look nothing alike. He's all light brown hair and sparkling eyes, while both her hair and eyes are as black as coal. "I overheard some boys on the football team discussing Amalie's new boyfriend. He doesn't really seem like her type, now does he?" She quirks one side of her lips, giving them a knowing look. If she's learned anything from her years forced into public school, it's that girls like Amalie and her friends thrive on gossip. She figures she can provide a little fuel, and hopefully, they'll erupt in gossip about her brother and Amalie, as their *kind* do.

The brunette's mouth puckers as if she's desperately trying to stop from spilling a secret... Or, as these...people...call it...*tea*. Lia has never understood that strange, uncouth nickname.

"What's your name?" Lia asks, scooting a fraction closer and plastering an unsuspecting smile on her face—a disarming technique she's learned from her father, her biggest role model.

The brunette grins, pleased to have the conversation switch briefly to herself. "My name is Tasha! I'm the head of the senior student council." She shrugs one shoulder lightly as if it's not that big of a deal, though, by the blush on her cheeks, she's only making a show of being humble. I make a *googly-awe* face and she caves, flashing a secretive glance toward Amalie and Henry before admitting, "Amalie *has* told us about him. Apparently, his name is Henry or Harry or something like that. He's really smart. Like…*Einstein* smart, according to Amalie."

"I didn't realize she likes boys who are smart," Lia adds, biting her lip in contemplation. What does his knowledge have to do with her infatuation?

"Yeah, but you see, Amalie is a senior this

year—and since we only have a term left before we graduate, she's in some serious trouble. She's failing her history class, and that's the last credit she needs to get her diploma," Tasha explains, wincing. "I feel so bad for the girl. But she figured out a super clever way to secure a passing grade. She's been flirting with that boy for weeks now and convincing him to do her homework." Tasha exchanges glances with her friends around her before leaning closer to Lia. "You can't tell a soul I said this. She would get in *so much* trouble, and that poor boy would probably get suspended too."

Lia sits up straighter, clenching her jaw. There's no way she's going to allow her little brother to get taken advantage of like this. And there's certainly no way she's going to let him get *suspended*. She has to do something about this...and fast.

She chuckles, shaking her head playfully—as she's seen numerous girls her age do. "No way! I won't tell a soul." Not a complete lie, Lia deduces. She won't tell a *human* soul, and that is surely what Tasha meant. However, the garter snakes that lurk in the bushes behind the gymnasium are fair play. "Now, if you will excuse me, I have to go find the bathroom."

Tasha crinkles her nose in disgust but doesn't say anything more, allowing Lia to stride across the bleachers, reveling in her forming plan. She will free her brother of Amalie's manipulating claws, even if it ends in Lia getting suspended instead.

The next day, after Lia and Amalie's physical education class, Lia puts her plan into action. Coiling around Lia's fisted hand is a green and black garter snake she found right outside. They're not venomous snakes, but someone like Amalie is sure to get a spook nonetheless. Amalie straightens up after pulling her clean shirt on, and that's when Lia reaches up and lets the slick creature slip down the back of Amalie's pink tank top. The cheerleader's screams start immediately, bringing a smile to Lia's face.

She finds it rather pleasant to watch her nemesis scream in absolute terror. That's what Amalie deserves for messing with Henry.

Amalie whirls around, and the snake slithers down her back and onto the floor, making a quick escape toward the cracked open doors. The screams of the rest of the girls in the locker room follow on its tail.

Amalie's face is waxen, and her eyes are blotchy and red from crying. She points an accusatory finger toward Lia, then shouts in an undignified and hysteric way: "This is *your* fault! *You* did that! Wait until the coach hears about this!" Following her rather hostile declarations, her bottom lip trembles and she bursts into another bout of terrified sobs.

Before someone can summon the coach, Lia slips through the door, following the snake into the golden sunshine. She has to go find her brother and explain the entire thing. She's wrought her revenge on the girl tampering with her brother's heart and stealing his knowledge, but now she has to face her brother's crushing disappointment. He'll be so heartbroken. Her brother has always been more...*emotional* than Lia. A trait that she's always seen as a weakness —but even if she doesn't agree with her brother's passionate emotions, it doesn't mean she wants to hurt him. If she could spare him the pain of Amalie's manipulation, then Lia would. She'd take it herself if she could.

She hastily leaves the campus, hoping she can put a good block between her and the school before the coach, the principal, and whatever other ghouls have been summoned can find her.

Henry smiles at Lia over the rim of his glass of lemonade. "Did your teacher let you out of class early too?" he asks, setting his glass down on the kitchen island and pouring his sister a glass out of the pitcher. He scoots it across the island toward Lia as she plops down on a barstool.

Lia returns a tight-lipped smile, not looking forward to breaking her brother's heart. She takes the glass of lemonade and sips at it genially, forming her confession in her mind. When she sets down the glass again, she clears her throat and begins: "Henry. I've noticed that Amalie has been paying a lot of attention to you recently. I found it odd, so I did some digging —"

Henry's brown eyes flash with anger and hurt. "Of course you find it odd. You can't picture anyone liking me, can you? Why can't you just let me be happy, Lia? Is that too much to ask? Or does your unhappiness have to rub off on me too?" He turns to storm from the room.

Lia drags her hand down her face in exasperation. *Of course* he took it out of context! Not that he's entirely wrong. Lia knows the Grimslis aren't a likable family, so imagining someone pushing that aside and choosing to like Henry does seem *wrong*. She finishes off her glass of lemonade, summoning her courage, then trails after Henry, taking the stairs up to his attic room two at a time. Henry never locks his door—since he doesn't believe in locking his family out—so she takes advantage of his trust and swings it open.

Henry's stroking the chords of his ukulele absentmindedly, a crease between his brows and a frown on his face. He glares up at Lia when his door hits the wall, knocking a vinyl record he has hung on his wall to the floor. "I don't want to hear your excuses, Lia."

Lia rolls her eyes. "You have to listen, Henry. My suspicions weren't unwarranted! I discovered something today when I was talking to her friends. Just hear me out, okay?"

He sighs, setting his ukulele on the bed

beside him. "Fine. Spit it out."

"Amalie is failing her history class and isn't going to graduate. She found out that you're incredibly smart—that's why she's been flirting with you and asking you to do all her homework." Lia crosses her arms, her eyes flitting over to his desk where multiple sheets of paper are strewn. Before he can respond, she crosses over to his desk and picks up the first sheet of paper as evidence. Amalie's name is sprawled across the top—the only thing on this page that's written in her hand. High school teachers don't pay enough attention to catch the slight shift in their handwriting, especially since Henry is mimicking her swirly letters and heart-shaped periods. "Really, Henry?" Lia sets the piece of paper back down.

Henry flushes. "How did you know I was doing her homework?"

"Her friends told me! That's the only reason she's even talking to you, Henry!"

"That's not true," he insists, turning the color of a tomato. "I can prove it."

Lia watches him doubtfully. "How?"

"She's at cheerleading practice right now. Let's go over there and ask her," Henry suggests, tightening the laces on his sneakers. He doesn't wait for Lia's response before trudging back down the stairs and out the front door.

Lia follows him into the warm spring air. She doubts this is going to help any—Amalie will just lie and accuse Lia of being a psychopath after the whole snake-down-shirt debacle comes to light. But if this is truly what Henry wants, then fine.

They walk the mile back to the high school in silence. Henry stews in his anger, while Lia mentally plots out an escape route if Amalie brings the principal in to detain her. It was only a garter snake, jeez.

When they reach the high school, they sneak around to the back entrance to the gymnasium, where cheerleading practice is typically held. Henry pushes open the cracked door to slip inside, his foot freezing mid-air. Lia lifts an eyebrow before peeking over his shoulder. On the opposite side of the gymnasium, Amalie, in all her blonde-braided glory, is engulfed in a rather passionate kiss with a football player. Henry backs a step away, rage erupting across his face. He lets the door close before they can be spotted.

"I told you," Lia says, as a dutiful sister should.

Henry turns toward her, his brown eyes growing darker as his rage crescendos into vengeance. "Fine. So, you were right. I was being used." He bites his lip as if merely saying it burns his tongue. "She won't get away with this."

Lia smiles. The Grimslis have always had a talent for wreaking revenge. "What would you like to do about it?"

"I happen to know that she's petrified of ants." He grins wickedly. "And I also happen to know that there's an anthill behind the bleachers on the football field, and where she's parked her car."

Lia claps him on the back. "This is much better than a snake."

He chuckles in bewilderment. "What snake?"

Later that night, Lia and Henry clink their lemonade glasses together as Amalie's throat-ravaging scream envelopes the entire town.

Brother Frankenstein

L ia Grimsli jolts up in bed, cold sweat slicks her forehead, gliding down her temple, as the ghost of her laugh runs through her mind again and again. Alongside the ghost of her brother's voice.

She glances across the room at the empty lone bed pushed flush against the wall, the navy sheets wrinkled. She drags a hand down her face and forces herself out of bed and onto her feet. She can't stay in bed all night, not when she has so many things to do.

Lia collects a fabric tie off her nightstand and wraps her hair—nearly as dark as the shadows surrounding her—away from her face. She slips into a pair of flats and runs a hand down her slightly ruffled dress. Lia hates to look untidy, especially in front of her brother, who always has his hair combed and his clothes ironed.

When she throws open the apartment door, she's greeted by Henry's ever-stoic face. She beams, wrapping her arm through his and helping him to his feet. His eyes—a light brown —stare back at her, but he doesn't seem particularly happy to see her.

"Are you ready, brother?" Lia asks, nudging him with her elbow. She's used to his silence— he's always been quiet, answering her instead with his weary expressions. "That's okay. It'll be just like last time."

She helps him into their bedroom, where she

pulls his comb from his nightstand and glides it through his thinning hair. "You look handsome. I'm glad you're visiting me again. You know you can always stay here with me. Your bed is where it's always been—exactly as you left it."

He drops his head onto her shoulder—and that's when she realizes…

"Oh, you must be tired! I'm sorry. This is the last time, I swear it. Then you can sleep as long as you want."

He gives her a look, which has her narrowing her eyes scornfully.

"I'm doing this for us, you know. You should be thanking me," she insists, returning the look ten-fold. He seems to understand, nesting his face in the crook of her neck.

Lia leaves him leaning against the wall beside her bed as she darts into their small closet, removing a charcoal-colored shoebox from the upper shelf. She sets it on the floor, takes the lid off, and pulls out two nearly identical parcels. She unwraps the first one, shredding the brown paper to the floor, and smiles at the kite. Her kite, to be exact. A gorgeous red kite with a stripe of white down the center. She tucks it under her arm before unwrapping the second parcel. Her brother's kite—a color resembling the night sky, freckled with white stars.

She slips it with hers under her arm as she returns to her brother, who's staring blankly at her bed—probably lost in thought again, as per his norm.

She helps him walk outside—where the sky is rolling with black clouds, hiding the stars. The sound of the beach a mile or so away crashes through the night—followed soon after by a streak of lightning striking the waves. The blinding white light reflects off the water, illuminating the beach and a row of abandoned apartments.

She's always appreciated that her and her brother's apartment is the only inhabited one, and has been for nearly a year, courtesy of Henry, of course. He's always had a flair for dramatics.

Lia shoots a glare at her brother as she tightens her arm around his waist, shifting him so the majority of his weight falls on her, and not his uncooperative legs.

The walk down to the shore is peaceful, increasingly so with every brilliant flash breaking up the night. Nature's exceptional orchestra—*crash, rumble, crash*—has been the constant undertone to all her favorite memories. Especially the memory of last year, a night just like this with the most spontaneous and striking display of nature's power. That night is her brother's most fond memory—she can just tell by the way he smiled, the way his face glowed, the way his eyes widened with each second. She's never seen her brother so happy before— so every storm since, she takes him back to the exact same spot on the exact same beach, just to see him smile like that again.

"Amazing, isn't it?" Lia whispers in awe, hardly able to peel her extraordinarily dark eyes away from the sky. She trains them on her brother instead, and his own expression, glossy eyes reflecting the light show. She must have a sixth sense, for she can tell exactly what he's feeling and thinking without uttering a word. Maybe it's the magic of siblinghood. Lia leans into his arms, soaking up the slightly musty scent that's prone to cling to him. She knows he lost something that night, one year ago. His ability to speak. Surely, the shock of beauty stole it from him. But that's fine, for a sister doesn't need to hear her brother speak to know what he wants to say. It hasn't affected him much, and he hasn't made any notion proclaiming himself unhappy.

A terrific bolt darts down from the heavens, spearing a humongous wave. The ring of white shoots from the spot in the water, clinging to the black rocks that peak above the ocean's surface.

Lia squeals with glee at the sight. "Would you look at that!" She claps her hands together, losing grip on her brother for half a second. He begins to crumple to the ground. She catches him, tugs him to her side, earning herself a tight-lipped smile. The kites flutter from under her arm to the ground, nestling among the small mounds of sand. Her feet, of their own volition, begin rocking back and forth with excitement. The midnight blue waves crawl closer to her feet as the main event draws closer as well.

"Any minute now," she exclaims, situating her brother. She holds him out in front of her— hands on his shoulders—and looks him up and down. "You look quite neat." She licks a thumb and wipes away a clump of dirt on his cheek, then runs her fingers through his hair. His skin appears particularly ashen, but that may be the fault of the moon more than his pallor.

She retrieves the kites from where they've fallen and unravels the strings from each. After the last failed attempt, nearly a month ago if she recalls correctly, she learned to line the string of the kite with a thin wire.

Her brother's excitement bounds off him like the waves against the rocks.

"I know, I know," Lia shouts, grinning. She

wraps the string of her kite around one of his hands, and the string of his own around his other hand, then watches them as they begin to dance on the strong winds.

This is the fourth or fifth kite she's gone through... All exactly identical to their originals, of course. Her brother wouldn't have it any other way.

"Any minute now," she repeats. Her voice is layered with expectation and anticipation as she begins to back up, feet then yards, and soon she's closer to the apartment than to her brother, who's slumped against the sand without her as support.

Suddenly, parting the sky in a glorious flash of blinding light is what they have both been waiting for...

The beach comes to life, yielding to the spectacular roar that rips through the air as the bolt of lightning strikes the kite, traveling down the wire at inhuman speed. Another bolt, seconds after the first, hits the next kite—burning them to crisps. Lia steps back. The current of electricity in the air frizzes her hair and makes her skin tingle.

Her brother glows—a glow replicating that of the first night, and that's when she knows that he is happy, *truly* happy.

His body shudders and a stench fills the air. But through it all, Lia can't wipe the grin from her face—for she knows this is what her brother wants, what she wants too… To finally see him in the same light she did all those months ago… and now, she can finally say the particularly macabre goodbye she's been waiting for, for the numerous times she's attempted to recreate that night nearly a year ago, she's failed. But not this time. This time it worked.

This time, as his body lurches off the ground, his ashen skin sizzling, his eyes wide and his smile wider, she knows she did it right.

BONUS STORY

This next story doesn't follow Lia or the Grimsli family, instead, it is a short story about young love and heartbreak that made my mother cry, so I figured it would be a disservice not to include it in my first collection.

-   Sincerely, Daphne

A Love Without Touch

It's been six months since I held his hand,
though not a day goes by that I don't try.
Vincent grins down at me. The brilliant rays of
the sun shine through his shoulder-length hair
and onto the patch of grass where I'm sitting.
He looks the same. Every day, I grow a little—
change a little. But he doesn't.

"How have you been, Ellie?" he asks,

sitting in front of me and leaning back against his headstone. He's still in his navy and white suit. The same suit he was wearing after our senior prom when he dropped me off at home and got back into his car... I glance away. The memory of him waving to me that final time will never leave me.

I dig my nails into my palms and force myself to meet his gaze. He looks so...alive. If the sunlight didn't shine through him instead of encompassing him, I'd be tempted to believe these past six months were just a nightmare. "I've been okay," I tell him, knowing that's what he wants to hear. Visiting him here...has helped me. But I just wish I could hold him one last time. Kiss him one last time.

He reaches toward me, his brow puckering with concern. As it always does, his hand falls through me, landing on the grass. He frowns. From this close, I can make out the specks of gold in his dark brown eyes. His thick black eyebrows lift, and he forces a smile to his face. "It will be okay, Ellie," he promises, tilting his head to study me. A dark curl flops across his forehead. Instinctively, I reach up to brush it behind his ear, but instead of touching his cheek, as I long to, it hovers mid-air.

My facade cracks, and tears escape from the corners of my eyes. "I hate this," I admit, trying to stop myself from crying. I wish I could feel his fingers entwined with mine, smell his coconut shampoo, or relax in the protection of his arms.

"I do too, Ellie," Vincent whispers, staring down at me with such an intense longing that my already broken heart shatters completely. "But this isn't forever."

I scrunch my face in confusion. "Isn't it? You're not truly here, Vincent. You're trapped…somewhere else, while I'm stuck without you."

He stands up, perching on the top of his headstone, one leg crossed under him while his other foot is flat on the ground. His headstone isn't elaborate. It's rectangular and made from light granite, with a dove carved on either side of his name. Every time I come down to the cemetery, I bring him a bundle of marigolds—his favorite—and tidy his grave. The marigolds are a lively contrast to the ghost standing before me. My eyes trace the jagged lines of his name, as they do every time I'm here, as if I'm convincing myself all this is real.

Vincent Heeler

2005 – 2024

Loving son and brother.

"There has to be something after death, Ellie," Vincent says, gesturing toward the cemetery that sprawls over the hillside of our small town. "How would you explain me if there wasn't?" He flashes his cocky smirk, which summons a chuckle from my lips. Despite the tears staining my cheeks and the ache in my chest, he still has the power to make me laugh... He still has the power to show me the good in situations. "And how would you explain that?" He turns to watch the sunset paint the sky in a rainbow of colors. "Haven't you heard the stories?"

I stand, dust off my jeans, and step up beside him. My eyes widen as fiery oranges blend into the light blue of day, inviting it to rest. Soft watercolor clouds dot the sky, tinted orange, pink, and purple as the sunlight fades. "I've heard stories that sunsets are your loved ones looking down on you, but they're just stories, Vincent," I declare, shaking my head despite my awe.

He gives me a look. "There's always a grain of truth in every story, Ellie."

"So, you're telling me that the sky is full of ghosts right now?" I raise an eyebrow, wanting to laugh at my question—but how can I laugh at such a thing, when my boyfriend who died six months ago is right beside me? Before his accident, I didn't believe in anything supernatural. But after, he presented me with the evidence to believe in otherworldly entities —to believe that there is so much more hidden in the fabric of the world, just waiting to be discovered.

His eyes crinkle with laughter. "Not exactly.

I like to think that it's their love shining down on you." He peers over at me, his eyes softening. "Love is a beautiful thing, after all, Ellie."

My heart stutters at his tone. Again, I want to turn toward him and kiss his cheek or take his hand in mine. But I can't. "I miss you so much. How am I supposed to continue without you?" Tears leak from my eyes and slide down my cheeks, landing on the blades of bright green grass at the base of his headstone. For the past year, I thought I was so lucky to have found "the one" at such a young age. I was so in love...I was blinded to the possibility of losing him. I pinch my eyes shut, trying to push away the image of his parents knocking on my door with their blotchy, tear-stricken faces and red eyes, sobbing as they told me about Vincent's accident. How he didn't survive the impact.

"I love you, Ellie," Vincent says, turning toward me and away from the sunset. He rests both his feet on the grass, still sitting on the top of his headstone, and intertwines his hands, dangling them between his legs. His dark eyes are glossy, but a knowing smile transforms his expression from sad to accepting. "I think it's time I go."

I shake my head, tears flowing freely down my face now. My voice wobbles as I insist, "You can't leave me, Vincent. Where will you go?"

Vincent blinks away a tear of his own, tilting his chin up to face the breathtaking sky blanketing us. "Up there, Ellie. You'll see my love in every sunset. In every streak of color in the sky."

"But—but you're the only one for me," I sob, shaking my head more frantically now.

Vincent sighs, shaking his head solemnly. "No, Ellie. You're the only one for me. Go live your beautiful life and find someone to share it with. I will never stop loving you. For eternity, I'll watch over you, reminding you of my love with every blooming flower and every sunset." He stands up from his perch on his headstone, lifting his hand to hover just beside my cheek.

"I will carry your love with me wherever I end up."

"Vin—" I choke out, blinking away my tears so I can devour the sight of him, engraving every freckle, every tuft of hair, every wrinkle in his suit into my memory, scared that I will forget something...forget him. "Please. I need you."

Vincent steps toward the sunset, reflecting the palette of colors in his dark eyes. "I will always be with you, Ellie. You'll carry me with you. Now go, live for the both of us." He juts his chin toward my silver Volkswagen, waiting on the gravel path bisecting sections of the cemetery. "You have so much ahead of you, and I feel blessed to have been a part of your life, no matter how small."

I reach toward him again, trying desperately to take his hand, to pin him to this earth beside me... But that would be cruel of me. I slowly retract my hand, watching him as he spins in a slow circle, staring up at the glory of the painted sky. He deserves to go somewhere beautiful...

To no longer be stuck in this cemetery, trapped on earth when he should be basking in the peace of the hereafter. His eyes find mine again as his body slowly disappears. With a final smile, he's gone.

I drop to my knees, shifting my gaze from the place he was just standing and up to the sky. Yellow and orange jut through the purple and pink of the sunset, encircling the sun like a wreath of petals. Marigold petals.

Tears shine in my eyes. I miss him with my entire heart, but at least now I know he's where he belongs.

The End

What to Read Next

Start _Kingdoms and Curses_ for a charming medieval fantasy adventure told in five short books. Each book follows a different character and their animal companion as they navigate witchcraft, royalty, and young love. This is a no spice, no cursing fantasy series perfect for upper middle grade to young adult readers.

Start _Emilia of the Solstice Realm_ for an action-packed, dark fantasy trilogy following a princess who lost her memory. These full-length high fantasy novels are perfect for young adult to new adult audiences. They have sweet romance (no spice) and little to no cursing. This trilogy is rich in fantasy lore and houses a vibrant world of mages, mermaids, vampires, yetis, shapeshifters, and so much more.

If you want a break from fantasy, read Daphne Paige's young adult thriller/murder mystery romance, _Jess_. _Jess_ is a short novel following a group of teens who live in a camp in the woods called The Scurry when one of them starts to pick the others off in the shadows…

Acknowledgments

Thank you for reading my little short story collection, and I hope I disturbed you and entertained you in equal parts.

There are several people who helped bring this book to life, or inspired parts of it.

Nonni and Mom, thank you from the bottom of my scary lil' heart for all your work on my books. You both make me a better writer—even if you do laugh at my writing right to my face 90% of the time.

Papa, for your constant spooky pictures you always send to the group chat and for reading my particularly ghoulish stories. I know you've already read a couple of these stories over the years, but I hope you enjoy the rest just as much.

Sydney, Jacob, and Doug, because I can't *not* mention you.

And Gimli. This is your empire, my baby.

About the Author

Daphne Paige has always loved writing; watching and learning from her mother, who's also a writer. With the majority of her time spent writing, the breaks between stories makes her remember she has an actual life away from her characters. During those breaks, she loves to play video games, hangout with her various pets, and watch classic black and white films with her family. Daphne lives in Oregon helping her family with their popcorn business.

Signed books: https://popcorn-publishing.com/

Connect with the author on social media:
Instagram: @daphne.paige.books
TikTok: @daphne.paige.books

More by the Author

Kingdoms and Curses:
The Heiress of Gaia
The Empire's Witch
The Prince of Klymora
The King's Sorcerer
(Book 5 Coming Soon...)

Emilia of the Solstice Realm:
Return of Eve
Banished by Darkness
(Book 3 Coming Soon...)

More:
Jess
The Macabre Life of Lia Grimsli
Forest of Monsters Novella (Coming Soon...)